DREAMWORKS

DRAGONS

HICCUP

AND FRIENDS

Popcorn
ELT
Readers

New Words

dragon

The **dragon** is big.

fire

The **fire** is hot.

fight

The boys are **fighting**.

fly

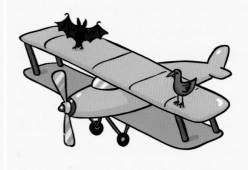

They can **fly**.

island

They live on an **island**.

strong

The man is **strong**.

leader

She's the **leader**!

Viking

They are **Vikings**.

Where's the popcorn?
Look in your book.
Can you find it?

I live on Berk. It is a small **island**.

Dragons come to the **island**. Some **Vikings fight** the **dragons** but I like them.

My dad's name is Stoick. He is the **leader** of all the **Vikings** on Berk.

Stoick

Snotlout

Snotlout is a **strong Viking.**

Fishlegs

Fishlegs understands a lot about **dragons**.

Tuffnut and Ruffnut
are brother and sister.

Tuffnut

Ruffnut

Gobber is my dad's friend. He is our teacher.

Gobber

Toothless

We all have **dragons**! Night Fury **dragons** are black. You can't see them at night.

Toothless is a Night Fury. He is my friend.
I **fly** on him.

Astrid has a Deadly Nadder **dragon**.
It is very quick. It is good at **fighting**.

Fishlegs **flies** on a Gronckle. Gronckles like to sleep. They eat a lot of rocks.

rock

Zippleback **dragons** have two heads. Tuffnut and Ruffnut **fly** and **fight** on a Zippleback.

Snotlout's **dragon** is a Monstrous Nightmare. It makes hot **fire**. It is an angry **dragon**.

The **Vikings** and **dragons** are friends.

How many **dragons** can you see?

THE END

After you read

1 Complete the sentences.

a) Hiccup lives

b) Stoick is

c) Hiccup can

d) Snotlout is a strong

e) Fishlegs and Snotlout are

i) Hiccup's friends.

ii) Viking.

iii) on a small island.

iv) fly on Toothless.

v) the leader of the Vikings.

2 Write the words.

Crossword:

```
            1
            v
2 [ ][ i ][ ]
            k
3       [ i ][ ][ ]
4 [ ][ ][ ][ n ]
   5 [ ][ ][ g ][ ]
```

3 Circle the correct words.

a) Dragons **come to** / **are** the island.
b) Gronckles like to **sleep** / **fight**.
c) Zipplebacks have two **hairs** / **heads**.
d) Monstrous Nightmare dragons **eat** / **make** hot fire.
e) You can't **see** / **listen to** a Night Fury at night.

4 Draw a dragon. What colour is it?

My dragon is ....

Quiz time!

Answer the questions. Yes or No?

		Yes	No
1)	Deadly Nadders are Vikings.	☐	☑
2)	Gobber is Hiccup's dad.	☐	☐
3)	Stoick is a teacher.	☐	☐
4)	Hiccup doesn't like Astrid.	☐	☐
5)	Hiccup likes dragons.	☐	☐

SCORES

How many of your answers are correct?

0–2: Read the book again! Can you answer the questions now?

3–4: Good work! You like Hiccup and Friends!

5: Wow! Are you a Viking?

Chant

1 **T 5** Listen and read.

Dragons

Zipplebacks have got two heads,
Deadly Nadders are blue,
Gronckles eat rocks,
There's one behind you.

Toothless is a black dragon,
You can't see him at night,
Hiccup likes his Night Fury,
They're friends and they don't fight.

2 **T 6** Say the chant.

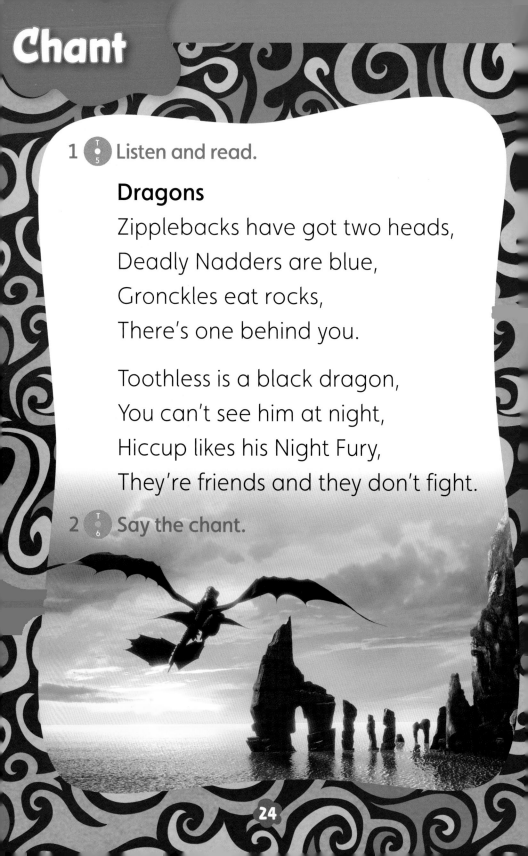